ER HARPER C
Harper, Charise Mericle,
author.
Wedgieman and the big bunny
trouble

Dear Parent:

Congratulations! Your child is taking the first steps on an exciting journey. The destination? Independent reading!

STEP INTO READING® will help your child get there. The program offers five steps to reading success. Each step includes fun stories and colorful art. There are also Step into Reading Sticker Books, Step into Reading Math Readers, Step into Reading Phonics Readers, Step into Reading Write-In Readers, and Step into Reading Phonics Boxed Sets—a complete literacy program with something for every child.

Learning to Read, Step by Step!

Ready to Read   Preschool–Kindergarten
• big type and easy words • rhyme and rhythm • picture clues
For children who know the alphabet and are eager to begin reading.

Reading with Help   Preschool–Grade 1
• basic vocabulary • short sentences • simple stories
For children who recognize familiar words and sound out new words with help.

Reading on Your Own   Grades 1–3
• engaging characters • easy-to-follow plots • popular topics
For children who are ready to read on their own.

Reading Paragraphs   Grades 2–3
• challenging vocabulary • short paragraphs • exciting stories
For newly independent readers who read simple sentences with confidence.

Ready for Chapters   Grades 2–4
• chapters • longer paragraphs • full-color art
For children who want to take the plunge into chapter books but still like colorful pictures.

STEP INTO READING® is designed to give every child a successful reading experience. The grade levels are only guides. Children can progress through the steps at their own speed, developing confidence in their reading, no matter what their grade.

Remember, a lifetime love of reading starts with a single step!

Visit us on the Web!
StepIntoReading.com
randomhouse.com/kids

Educators and librarians, for a variety of teaching tools, visit us at
RHTeachersLibrarians.com

Library of Congress Cataloging-in-Publication Data
Harper, Charise Mericle.
Wedgieman and the big bunny trouble / by Charise Mericle Harper ; illustrated by Bob Shea.
    pages cm. — "A Step 3 reader."
Summary: "When Bad Dude creates a machine that makes objects grow enormously or shrink to tiny size, it's up to Wedgieman to straighten things out." — Provided by publisher.
ISBN 978-0-307-93073-6 (trade) — ISBN 978-0-375-97060-3 (lib. bdg.) —
ISBN 978-0-307-97424-2 (ebook)
[1. Superheroes—Fiction. 2. Inventors—Fiction. 3. Size—Fiction. 4. Humorous stories.]
I. Shea, Bob, illustrator. II. Title.
PZ7.H231323Weg 2013 [E]—dc23 2012043053

Printed in the United States of America   10 9 8 7 6 5 4 3 2 1

WEDGIEMAN
and the
BIG BUNNY TROUBLE

By Charise Mericle Harper
Illustrated by Bob Shea

Random House 🏠 New York

There was a new superhero in town.

His real name was Veggieman,

but the children called him Wedgieman.

Wedgieman could do lots of things.

Right now he was fixing
his outfit.
He was making a pocket.
And he was changing
his Veggieman name
into a Wedgieman name.
He pulled the V off
his suit and put on a W.

"This will make the children happy,"
said Wedgieman.
Wedgieman cared about the children
more than he cared about his own name.
Wedgieman was a real hero.

Wedgieman put the V in his pocket.
"I might need to change back
into Veggieman," he said.
He thought about a vegetable emergency.
He smiled.
Now he was ready for anything.

Bad Dude was not a hero.

Bad Dude was a bad guy.

He had all kinds of bad-guy stuff:

a secret hideout,

an evil laugh,

super inventor skills,

and lots of plans

to take over the world.

Bad Dude was proud of his
newest invention.

The Powerful Ordinary-Object Phaser,
or P.O.O.P. for short,
was a zapping machine.

It made things bigger and smaller.

He smiled and patted the P.O.O.P.

Bad Dude picked up a small box.

"Buzz," went the box.

"Hello, bee," said Bad Dude.

"Soon you will be a giant bee!"

He laughed his evil laugh

and opened the box.

The bee flew out the window.

It scared a cute bunny.

The bunny ran in front of the zapper.

"Aaaah, Giant Cute Bunny!"
screamed Bad Dude.

Bad Dude did not like bunnies.

They were too furry and too cute.

Bad Dude opened the door

to his hideout.

"Beat it, bunny! Shoo!" said Bad Dude.

"Growl," said the giant bunny's tummy.

The bunny was hungry.

It wanted to eat.

It did not want

to go away.

The giant bunny hopped

all over the room looking for food.

A giant bunny in a secret hideout

is not a good thing.

GROWL

The bunny knocked over
bottles of goo,
boxes of gadgets,
and even Bad Dude's favorite chair.
The secret hideout was a mess!
It was a disaster.

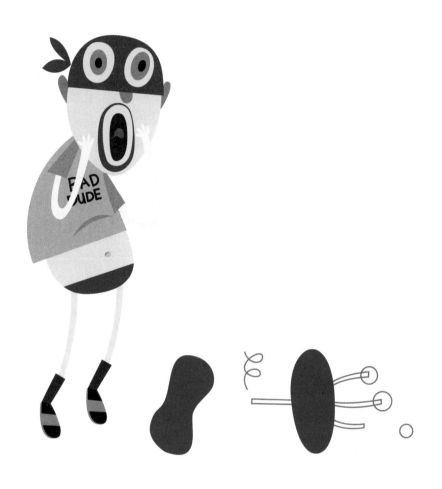

"Noooooooo!" shouted Bad Dude.

He loved his special chair,

and now it was broken.

Bad Dude yelled
at the bunny.
What he said
was not very nice.

The bunny hopped on
top of Bad Dude.
Bad Dude was
trapped under four
giant furry paws.

"I'm stuck!"
cried Bad Dude.

He waved his arms in the air.

His hand hit the bee.

It stung his finger.

"Owwwww!" screamed Bad Dude.

Everyone in town heard the scream.

Wedgieman ran.

The children ran.

Wedgieman got there first.

"Cute bunny," said Wedgieman.

"Growl," said the bunny's tummy.

"Feed it something!" screamed Bad Dude.

Wedgieman looked in his pocket.

He took out two coins, a V,

and three baby carrots.

"Pick the carrots!" shouted Bad Dude.

"Zap them with the P.O.O.P.!

It will make them bigger!"

Bad Dude pointed to the P.O.O.P.

with his giant finger.

Wedgieman aimed the machine
at the carrots.
He pressed the button.

ZAP! The carrots were huge!

"Wow," said Wedgieman.

"That looks impressive—and delicious!"

The bunny thought so, too.

It hopped over to eat a carrot.

Bad Dude was free.

Bad Dude ran
to the zapper and pushed
a different button.
ZAP!

The bunny was small again.

"Now it's even cuter," said Wedgieman.

He went over to give the bunny a pat.

"Perfect!" said Bad Dude.

He pointed the P.O.O.P.

right at Wedgieman.

"Now it's your turn to be small!"

said Bad Dude.

He put his head back

and laughed his evil laugh.

"Not so fast," said Wedgieman.

He turned and kicked the machine.

It spun around and knocked
Bad Dude to the ground.

There was a fight.

Crash! Owww! My finger! Smash! Eeeee!

My finger! Clunk! Yeeowww! My finger!

The giant zapper was broken.

Bad Dude was tied up.

Wedgieman was the winner.

THE END—OR IS IT?

Wedgieman checked his costume.

Everything looked perfect.

He was ready for the children.

"Giant carrots for everyone!"
shouted Wedgieman.

"Yay! Wedgieman!" cheered the children.
"Our hero!"

The carrots were delicious.
When they were gone,
it was time to take
Bad Dude to jail.
Wedgieman knew
there was one thing left to do.

The children knew, too.

"Give yourself a wedgie!" they shouted.

"Okay," said Wedgieman.

He gave himself a wedgie.

"That was the Giant Carrot Wedgie!"

shouted Wedgieman.

"YAY!" screamed the children.

Wedgieman smiled.

He picked up Bad Dude

and jumped into the sky.

"Aaaah!" screamed Bad Dude.

He was not used to sky travel.

"I love wedgies!" said a girl.

The children smiled.

"That was a good one,"
said a small boy.

He was right.

It was.